Denying the Faith

Errol O'Neill

Denying the Faith

& other stories

Denying the Faith & other stories
ISBN 978 1 74027 757 0
Copyright © text Errol O'Neill 2012
Cover photograph: Richard Jones

First published 2012
Reprinted 2016

Ginninderra Press
PO Box 3461 Port Adelaide 5015
www.ginninderrapress.com.au

Contents

This Clown

On the school tennis courts one afternoon back in sepia memory, I was performing the role of ball boy. I was not playing tennis and scoring points, and working up a healthy sweat. No, that would have been unlikely, as the untalented and the talented in the realm of sport were early sorted out and I was definitely not among the latter. Was I there because I was supposed to be playing tennis and when I got to the court the inevitable happened and I was knocked out of some compulsory serial competition early? Not likely, but possible. Was it just assumed that I was no good at the game and was expected to be ball boy for the more serious tennis-playing boys?

Memory cannot answer all these questions but it does show that at some point I was standing there, having collected some tennis balls at the periphery, holding three in my hand and not having a clear idea of what to do with them.

Father O'Madden came down to supervise. He saw some kids standing around not playing when they should have been playing and called out to them. Why are you just standing there, lads?

We haven't got any balls, Father.

He looks around and sees me standing there with three in my hand, caught, as I always recall it, in a frozen-forever, Grecian urn moment. Is this a moment of artistic wonder, glazed, and in glorious colour, unchangeable, for all future generations to admire? No. Is this an innocent boy such as Augustine might discover on the beach, not filling holes with sea water but with the symbol of the Trinity in his hand, causing even holy sages to stop and reflect on things eternal? No.

This clown here has three of them! O'Madden exclaims.

Several elements, caught in a moment, a glass-mounted split-second which I have slid under the microscope many times over the years in order to analyse. Not only the visuals, but also the psychology of the incident. The visuals were pretty ordinary. Anyone walking past would have seen nothing extreme. No violence, no shouting, no obvious signs of distress or torment. Just a plain after-school scene with boys and a teacher on the tennis courts. But the psychology written into this moment has taken some years to analyse.

A scene with three parts.

The first part is me standing there with three tennis balls. These were the days when tennis balls were white, not yellow like they are today. I wasn't thinking too much about what I was doing, just standing there holding the balls. Right hand, left hand, I don't remember, but from memory all in one hand. I might well have been amazed to find that I could hold three balls in one hand and got so amused by this that I lost concentration on the job I was supposed to be doing. Which was making sure the real tennis players were kept supplied with balls so they could ace one another and demonstrate their sporting ability, and maybe one day follow Hoad and Emerson into noble immortality.

The second part is O'Madden, close by, so that he doesn't have to shift his gaze much from the direction of the non-playing boys. He would have looked over at them and seen they were not playing as they should have been, and shouted out immediately, Why aren't you boys playing? And their No balls reply came quickly. Then with a slight turn of his head, O'Madden is able to see me close by with the balls in hand, and then he issues his peremptory derogation. This Clown. He probably didn't think much about his choice of words; he was just managing the tennis court as he did after school four days a week, making sure the balls which had come off the court got back to the serving end. But the balls weren't just lying on the ground and he didn't have to direct someone to pick them up and throw them to the other end of the court, he had a perfectly evident reason that the balls were stopped in their trajectory. It was This Clown. This Clown had intervened to stop the serious business of tennis playing. The serious business of keeping young boys busy so that they didn't have time to think lewd thoughts. And it was a perfect situation in which to have lewd thoughts. Here was someone saying, We haven't got any balls, Father. An ideal opportunity to make jokes and indulge in sniggering. But this is serious tennis business. Serious sportsmen don't make jokes about testicles.

The third part is the innocent, nameless, faceless boys of memory, who should have been advancing every moment towards their place in the Davis Cup, standing idle.

This depiction of the three unlikely estates of this realm looks ordinary enough on the storyboard. Now, let's get the camera rolling. Here is the black-robed priest with the roman collar and the rimless Irish priest glasses. A slight turn of the head, sufficient to see the Clown, the commoner, the spanner in the works, the one stopping progress through his utter foolishness, his dawdling, his complete lack of ability to take life seriously and work for the common good. Close-up on the symbol of the Trinity in his idle and useless hand. Intercut with a long shot of the tennis-playing boys at the other end of the court, waiting patiently, racquets in hand, no balls. Now back for a mid-shot – a slight look of exasperation, even anger, on the face of the priest. This completes the simple visual outlay for this memory. Now to the darker, internal aspects.

Father O'Madden didn't say to me, Would you please throw those balls over to so and so and let them continue their game. No, he said, This Clown here has three of them. This Clown, not my name. That was the barb. That was the epithet. It all fitted in – only a clown would have no ability for sport, only a clown would be standing there stupidly, not realising that serious tennis players need to be constantly supplied with the stuff of their game in order to fulfil their role as elite sportsmen. The three estates, as ordained from the beginning, must know their place and work in harmony to keep society functioning in the proper way.

All right, Father O'Madden, let me now virtually but of course fruitlessly interrogate you across time and space. What did you do after that incident? Did you go back to the priory and recite your Latin breviary and get ready for dinner and forget about that troubled tennis court assembly altogether, and forget about That Clown?

Well, I'm afraid I didn't do any of those things. I filed it all away. I filed away the ridicule in front of my peers, the implicit contempt, and particularly the concept of clown. Years later, in another phase of learning, and with an acquired appreciation of contradiction, irony and satire, I was to overturn the resentment of that incident and understand that to be a clown was to pursue a noble art.

But for many years after that day on the tennis court, clown was simply a tag for all the confusion and self-reproach that came naturally to an awkward, impressionable adolescent in the thrall of black-robed men. Whatever a priest said was true. If you were absolved of your sins by a priest, you could relax and feel happy, knowing that your soul had been washed whiter than white. If a priest taught you how to solve a problem in geometry, you could be assured that the knowledge he imparted was correct and would be correct for all time. If a priest told you or, more insultingly, told others that you were a clown, then that must also be true.

The truth and power of that moment persisted in some way. Even when I heard in later life that O'Madden had left the priesthood and run off with the housekeeper, I understood perfectly and instantly why he might have done so, and didn't condemn him. But I still couldn't grant him absolution. In response to the opprobrium he offered that day I could only silently swear an ominous tennis court oath on behalf of myself and all the others suffering under the old regime which would in time, and in a convoluted sense, bring about a revolution.

Denying the Faith

It was a hot Saturday arvo. My brother and I were minding our own business, sitting on the steps of Stewart's department store at Stones Corner.

We were minding our own business, but he came over. He was big and aggressive, and he had that cheeky look that was obligatory for state school kids in those days. At least this was the notion of state school kids which a convent school kid like myself was obliged to hold without question.

One look at his sweaty, unkempt appearance told me that he'd probably just finished a hot, dusty cricket game, or some act of wanton cruelty, like hurling stones at the waterfowl in the creek behind the municipal library.

'Youse play cricket?' He stood provocatively before us, demand-ing an answer as if it was his right.

My brother didn't feel inclined to reply. There comes a certain aloofness which you can use with impunity when you're older than another kid, and he was exercising it. This was the law of the streets.

But I felt that I should reply, seeing this kid was more my contemporary. Someone had to do something, anyway, because he was staring at me and I knew he wouldn't go away until he got an answer.

'Yeah…a bit,' I said, not wanting to let on that I detested the game as if it were the work of Satan himself. I was aware of the dirt in the creases of his elbows being turned into mud by his perspiration.

The smell of his breath, his flushed face and his unwanted attention were becoming oppressive. It seemed he would undoubtedly grow up to be one of the red-faced drunks you saw staggering out of the pub across the road every afternoon. They wore short-sleeved shirts, fawn trousers and grey Akubras, and had rolled-up *Telegraph* form guides stuffed in their back pockets. There was a virtual army of such persons inhabiting the streets of Stones Corner during my childhood. Sitting here, on the steps of Stewart's store, I could look across the road and see them, and hear the race calls on the radio which emanated from the public bar along with the shouting and swearing and laughter of these red-faced men.

Walking past the pub was always difficult and I would avoid it if I could, preferring to walk on the other side of the road. If I did stray to the wrong side of the tram tracks, this army of drunks, it seemed, had orders to stumble out of the doorway just as I passed. Creatures of the nether world, surrounded by a toxic odour of stale beer, urine and vomit which they seemed to carry with them like a defensive shield, they would reach out with hairy arms. As their bloodshot eyes focused on my frail form, my terror would cause me to see them clutching at me and grabbing at me as they tried to drag me below into their pit of horror and despair.

I would sidestep, heart beating fast with fear. Then, to my relief, I would realise they weren't after me at all as I saw them embrace the familiar stability of a lamp post. An uncertain foot would stab at the ground until it was surely placed, the arm would remain around the post, then gradually, a sighting of the next lamp post would be made, distance from here to there calculated, and the drunk would teeter off, desperately trying to coordinate his limbs and movements with the mobile world around him. Where's the tram stop? Where's the cab rank?

As far as I knew, to become one of these eyeless, legless soldiers of misfortune was the natural fate of state school kids. I was thankful that I was taught by nuns, and prayed constantly that I would not grow up to become a Stones Corner Drunk.

'What's your highest score?' was this state school kid's next question.

I was stumped. It was bad enough telling what my parents called a white lie in the first place, giving him the impression that I liked the game. Now I would have to lie outright if I didn't want this grand inquisitor to know that my highest cricket score was a duck. For that was the truth. I had never made one single run in all those hated school matches which had me standing in the boiling sun for hour after hour. No balls were ever hit in my direction when I was fielding, and when I finally got to bat (the single moment of action in a day of otherwise complete emotional and intellectual torpor) the first ball would whiz past and knock the bails off before I could even register which end the bowler was coming from.

As he waited for my reply, he exercised his bowling arm. The dirt in the crease of his elbow seemed for a moment to contain more menace than his voice as he rolled imaginary balls out on to the tram lines of Logan Road. I found myself instinctively feeling my own elbow creases to confirm that they were not dirty, like his. I began to sweat.

Finally, my brother decided to forego his right to aloofness. 'What's your highest score?' he asked, without looking directly at the enemy. He was pretending to be engrossed in a Monopoly game in Stewart's window.

I was impressed with his tactic of pretended nonchalance.

'I asked youse first,' was the cricketer's indignant riposte.

'We don't have to answer if we don't want to,' said my brother, continuing the ploy of feigned indifference to this ruffian who was obviously beneath our contempt.

I was relieved to be out of the direct line of fire and I was enjoying the debate about rights and obligations. I was not previously aware that you could handle such attacks in this way, assuming that state school kids were the natural rulers of the streets and there was no escaping their demands.

'What are you? Chicken?' His bowling action slowed to a threatening halt.

'It's none of your business,' I said, with growing confidence. I had once heard this saying used in the playground to stunning effect, and never thought I would get the chance to repeat it, let alone use it to save my honour and, who knows, perhaps my life.

'What?' said the sweaty mischief-maker, as if I was speaking another language.

'It's none of your…bloody business,' I repeated, this time adding a swearword so he would realise I was just as tough as he was.

The argument had reached a plateau. I had defended my right to privacy, kept an intruder from getting access to information injurious to my sporting reputation, had avoided getting my nose bloodied, and had generally shown up this state school kid for the bully he was. The price that had to be paid was getting down into the gutter with him, of course, and using the kind of language such a ruffian himself would use. Still, it was a mild swearword, unlike some of the words which I had seen scrawled under the Stones Corner bridge and would never dare use in public – or private.

As Logan Road entered Stones Corner it became a bridge over an irregular and eccentric waterway. Upstream of the bridge, the waterway was more or less a large, open storm water drain. Below the bridge it turned into a chain of potholes and wetlands which spread across a large flat swamp area and provided a haven for many waterbirds as it meandered behind the library and the light industrial area which fringed the village centre at the junction of Logan and Old Cleveland Roads.

Somewhere beyond Stones Corner – beyond the boundaries of the known world, I had been told – this water eventually became part of the Brisbane River. In my adventurous imaginings, I planned to get a canoe and travel these lower reaches and then return like the famous explorers of old to confirm to all of Stones Corner that there was a real world beyond. If there was.

This waterway, which ran through the vast parkland which divided Stones Corner from Buranda, and which we honoured with the title Norman Creek, periodically overflowed after heavy rain and flooded low-lying backyards and some of the houses which weren't built on high stumps. My aunts' shopfront house was one of these. Some of my earliest memories are tinged with the smell of post-diluvial mud.

My brother and I often made fishing lines out of string and bent pins, and caught eels in this very stream, sitting very gingerly on top of the open concrete conduit in the reach above the bridge.

Under the bridge and behind the library were two places we were generally forbidden to go. We never really wanted to, anyway. But this forbidden territory, particularly under the bridge, is where the low life, including state school kids, congregated and left their shocking messages for other more innocent minds to discover.

It was under the bridge that, on a rare illicit venture into the demi-monde, I first saw the written version of the word 'fucking' scrawled across a wall in big black letters. However, it was misspelt as 'fucken' and was being used to qualify a noun. This shameful display (a later generation would recognise it as graffiti and analyse it in sociological and demographic terms) was obviously the work of state school kids, as it was both dirty language and bad spelling.

I have forgotten that particular noun, but for many years I saw the other word simply as an adjective. I was to learn much later in life that we were dealing with the present participle 'fucking' which had dropped its g and enlisted an apostrophe during centuries of colloquial employment as a metaphorical, descriptive term. To be correct, the word should have been spelt 'fuckin''. But such toughs as state school kids were bound to miss this fine point of grammatical inflection.

As I grew more familiar with the outward appearance of this kid confronting me outside Stewart's department store on this hot Saturday afternoon, it was clear to me that he was of the type that not only stoned the egrets in the creek behind the library but would have also been likely to write such obscenities on the wall under the bridge.

And so, attempting to rebut his advances, I had only used the mild 'bloody'. I didn't tell this state school kid to mind his own 'fuckin'' business. That might indeed have got me a bloody nose.

But oh, the power of controlled swearing! We had this hooligan beaten, I was sure. I looked to my brother for some sort of congratulation, but his tactic of cool unconcern had taken him a few steps away to look at a display of grey cardigans. Hardly convincing.

The intruder's aggression was not abating. He came even closer, the beads of perspiration on his face and his steadfast stare confirming his determination not to be denied.

Up to now, in the eyes of an imagined neutral observer, he had just been an average suburban kid hanging about on a lazy weekend, trying to make conversation with a couple of other kids whom he presumed were pretty much like himself. We could have simply answered his questions with the same sort of aggressive indifference and contempt he'd shown us, and he might have gone on his way.

But it was not to be.

'Tell me what your highest score is,' he insisted.

He leaned towards me, put his finger under the shoulder strap of my singlet, and pulled it up. The bottom of my singlet came out of my shorts. He let go, but noticed the brown cord of the scapular round my neck. He fished it out and sneered at the rectangular tag on the end of it. Confronted by the image of the Blessed Virgin appearing to St Simon Stock in 1251, he was at first perplexed, then amused.

He put two and two together. 'You a Catholic, mate?' he said with a mixture of disgust, curiosity and ridicule, which I had always known characterised the attitude of state school kids to religion.

This was the moment of truth. I knew instinctively that it was a moment that mattered a great deal. I could misrepresent my interest in cricket, or mouth the utmost nonsense about the mundane affairs of everyday life, or even utter the most foul swearwords in the hearing of others. All of that could be forgiven. But my response to his ridicule of religion was not in the same category. Now I was being called on to make a stand. This was the fundamental Yes or No. This was the moment after which the cock's crow would take on more significance than the condemnation of the highest earthly court. The moment that would lead to either perdition for all time or the ecstatic rapture of martyrdom. This was the moment the priests and nuns and the catechism has been preparing me for, all my nine long years. This was the moment of affirming, or denying, the faith itself.

I didn't deliberate long. No sooner had he posed the fateful question, 'You a Catholic, mate?', than I answered, 'Nah...'

I hardly knew what I was saying or why, at the time. All I knew was that I was being stood over by Attila the Hun, who would probably hit me with his sweaty Protestant fist if I answered yes. The simplest way to avoid being hit – or worse, despised – was to say no.

He mumbled some profanity, disdainfully flicked the tag at the end of my scapular with his grubby fingers, sending poor old Simon into a twirl, poked me in the chest for good measure, and sauntered off, practising his bodyline bowling at the motorman of a passing tram.

I was safe for the time being. I had discovered the principle of keeping out of trouble. I had learned the great lesson of expediency. It was indeed the moment of truth.

I turned to my brother with an air of smug satisfaction. But he didn't look pleased as he left the grey cardigans and walked over to me.

'Did you say you weren't a Catholic?'

'Yeah, but I...' My voice trailed off. I was overcome with confusion and guilt. As soon as I tried to excuse myself, I knew I had done wrong. My stomach and my bowels were in turmoil.

I hadn't recognised persecution when it came to me. I had expected it to be different. I had expected the path of heroism to be brightly lit, signs pointing the way. The persecutors would at least be dressed in military uniforms, speaking in thick foreign accents. To fill out the profile the nuns had given me, they would be Slavic, or possibly North Korean. An essential part of the background to this act of apostasy would be knives, guns, whips, the rack, dungeons, clanking chains. I mean, you would definitely know you were being persecuted for the faith. You would have a clear choice: fall down and worship this false idol, and your life will be spared; refuse to submit to our pagan gods and you will be taken out immediately to meet your death.

I had notionally rehearsed this scene a million times in my head. Death was the one I was supposed to choose. Glorious death, to which I would walk with great dignity, disregarding the sneers and taunts of the faithless crowd. Glorious death, no matter how horrible, after which I would be taken straight into the bosom of Abraham. I'd even be assured of skipping purgatory with such a death.

But a state school kid on Saturday arvo, ten minutes' walk from the parish church? How was it possible to recognise persecution there? How was it possible to know which false idol I was being asked to genuflect to?

All my attempts to justify my denial were hollow. I stood accused and condemned by my own words, by my own lack of courage and conviction. An object of public shame. State school kids were right to ridicule such a traitor as me.

'I thought he might hit me,' I protested weakly. Did I hear the sound of a rooster crowing somewhere beyond Logan Road? Or was it just the Hun back behind the library by now, stoning another shag?

'He wouldn't have hit you,' said my brother.

His scapular was well hidden under his singlet. He hadn't been close, like I'd been, to the horror of annihilation.

'Come on,' he said, 'Mum'll have tea on soon. Let's go home.'

That was the most powerful advice I had received that day, and it was the kind of advice that always brought me back to reality. We set off for home, discovering, to our surprise, that the savage barbarian himself was not back behind the library but walking along the opposite side of Old Cleveland Road.

Compared with torture and death on the rack, I had got off pretty lightly. But as we walked home along that very public footpath, on the long haul up to Coorparoo, following that unlikely tormentor (at a safe distance), there was pain enough.

He caught sight of us as he turned off and gave us one last derisory sneer before going home, where his mum was probably also getting tea ready. As he faded out of sight I knew my public shame would die away as well. But my private guilt had yet to run its long and instructive course.

Years later, I was standing in protest with many other believers on a public footpath outside an electricity depot in Taringa, where scabs were trying to break a strike. As the uniformed protectors of the established order approached us, I knew that it was not only possible, but also essential, to refuse to worship the false idol.

Going to Kanga's

Five minutes past six, Sunday evening. I'm cruising along Samford Road looking for a fare as I make my way back towards the city.

A hundred yards from the Alderley Arms hotel a mad, drunken wave catches my eye. He signals for me to make a U-turn. I don't want to, but a sudden break in the traffic makes it possible. He stands guard over one and a half cartons of beer beside him on the footpath. Tallies, not stubbies.

He points to them and nods at me. 'Got some piss here, driver. And there's another bloke comin',' he says anxiously.

I can appreciate his telling me about the other passenger, but I can't see why he tells me about the beer when it's quite obvious. Perhaps he wants me to help him put the beer in the boot. I pull the lever under my seat and the boot pops open. No way I'm getting out to help him.

'No, not the boot, mate. I'll put 'em on the back seat.'

Great. Now I have to get out and close the boot. 'Hurry up, mate. I can't park here.'

A bus screams past in the narrow space between my cab and the traffic island.

'She's right, china. He's just havin' a piss.'

He carries the beer awkwardly over to the car and tries to open the door with his knee. For the sake of public relations and in the interests of a pleasant journey, I decide to do a circumnavigation and open the door for him on my way back to the driver's seat. It always pays to be courteous to passengers who've been drinking and look set to continue drinking. It lessens the chance they'll turn nasty, or whinge when it comes time to pay the fare.

He almost drops the beer as he transfers it from the footpath to the back seat, but with a few quick and awkward grabbing actions he saves the precious cargo and places it carefully in the middle of the back seat. He sits beside it, wet and smelling of alcohol. He looks as though someone threw a glass of beer over him. Or he tried to urinate standing on his head.

He makes an attempt to strap the beer in, but it's only a lap seat belt and won't do the job. He thinks about shifting the grog to the outside so he can hold the half carton and the full carton together by means of the shoulder strap, but this looks like too much trouble. 'Bugger it, I'll just hold the bastards,' he mutters.

'Where are you going?' I ask.

'Into town, mate. Come on, shithead!'

For a second I think he's directing these last words at me, then I see his companion rushing out of the pub. He's an older man, fly undone, wearing brown, horn-rimmed glasses.

'Hold on, Bert. Clarrie's comin' after all,' the new arrival says, then he goes round the car and gets in the back seat, with the beer between him and the wet man.

'Jesus, I wish he'd make up his fuckin' mind! He said he was gonna piss off,' moans Bert.

Their friend Clarrie soon comes out of the pub, gets in the front seat, and we're off.

After a silence, Bert says to the other man in the back, 'Whaddya reckon about her, Ted?'

'She's a fuckin' moll,' replies Ted. 'They're all the same. Did you see the way she played up to me when he went out to have a piss?'

'What, Ernie's her old man, is he?' asks Clarrie, making a half-hearted attempt to find the front seat belt.

'Yeah,' replies Bert.

'Oh,' says Clarrie, 'news to me. I thought I was in with a chance.'

'She's got a decent-size coupla norks on 'er,' adds Bert.

'She's a fuckin' moll,' concludes Ted, with authority.

Another short silence.

'What part of town are you going to?' I ask.

Somebody behind me says, 'Spring Hill,' just as a hoon chops lanes in front of me, forcing me to brake suddenly.

'Steady on, driver. Got bottles here,' cautions Bert as he mothers his eighteen rattling babies.

'What about Skunk?' asks Clarrie, turning to his friends. 'I thought youse were goin' to Skunk's place.'

'No, we're goin' to Kanga's.'

'That dickhead? Let me out now,' complains Clarrie.

'I thought he was your best mate,' suggests Bert.

'What part of Spring Hill's he in? Still in that shit-hole off the laneway behind Boundary Street?'

'He's got a nice little set-up there,' says Ted.

'Well, let's stop and pick up Skunk on the way.'

'All right, but if he's not ready we're not waitin' for the prick.'

'Do you know Eureka Street, Kelvin Grove, driver? Just wanna stop there for a minute,' Clarrie says to me as the two in the back murmur on about the relative merits of having Skunk and Kanga under one roof.

'Remember that time they had that fight over that bottle of scotch? Jeez…'

'Fuckin' grog,' reflects Clarrie in the front seat, 'I'm sick of drinkin' the cunt… Told myself I wouldn't go to the Sunday session ever again, and look, where am I? Coulda stayed home, coulda visited me mum. But no. Going to drink piss with these bastards and the meanest mongrel this side of the equator. The almighty fuckin' grog.' He turns to me. 'A man's a fuckin' rat, driver, you know that? A man is a fuckin' rat.'

'You're not wrong, mate,' I offer, sympathetically.

'I can remember bein' taught at school that man is supreme in the animal kingdom, but I reckon the longer I live, the more I see the opposite. No, I mean, a man is a fuckin' rat, you know what I mean?'

Memo to all school principals. Legislation has been passed by the Queensland Parliament to ensure that a man is no longer a man but a rat, and must be seen to be a rat. Children must be taught the new evolutionary doctrine and the department will impose heavy fines on all teachers who continue to profess or teach anything to the contrary. The State Government Insurance Office clock will be relieved of its time-telling duties for a month while the lights are re-arranged to read 'Darwin was wrong. A Man's a fuckin' rat.'

'I mean, how did I get mixed up with this lot?' Clarrie continues, jerking a thumb towards the men and the beer in the back seat.

The two in the back are having an argument about the eighteen tallies, so they don't particularly notice that Clarrie is talking about them disparagingly.

'See what I mean? Only interested in the piss… A fuckin' rat.'

I've begun to warm to Clarrie's sense of humour. His critical observations on their current endeavour make me feel that at least he will be spared from the descent into rodent hell. Clarrie falls silent as the quarrel in the back seat gets more heated.

'I bought half of 'em.'

'You bought a third of 'em, Ted.'

'I bought a third of 'em too,' adds Clarrie, equal among rats.

'I haven't seen the colour of your money yet,' says Bert, in the aggressive tones of an ambiguous friendship.

'You'll get it, mate. Soon as the banks open tomorrow. Have I ever let you down?'

A sudden burst of mocking laughter from Ted, which eases the tension. Conveniently, for I was just beginning to feel guilty for not putting up my share. After eight hours on the road, your passengers can easily make you feel responsible for their lives. You sometimes have to hum or whistle in counterpoint to their conversation to remind yourself and them that you owe them nothing.

When we get to Eureka Street, Clarrie directs me to a block of flats.

Bert is looking after the beer, so he feels justified sending Clarrie in. 'Get 'im outa fuckin' bed and tell 'im to come an' 'elp us drink this fuckin' piss!'

I feel embarrassed by Bert's exaggerated enthusiasm and gaiety so I start to whistle a vague tune and slide back into my own world. Eureka Street, Kelvin Grove. Dropping a passenger here one night in 1972, I first heard the news of Whitlam's victory in the federal election. Twenty-three years of conservative rule ended and a new era of reform about to begin. 'Any election results?' some driver had enquired on the two-way. 'Yes,' replied the operator, 'It seems to be Gough by a long nose, driver.' I remember tingling all over as I stopped at the end of the street, wondering where to go to share the excitement. A new era dawning. New discoveries to be made. I summoned Archimedes. 'Eureka!' I shouted as I saw the street sign, and began to laugh. Peter Lalor, Chips Rafferty, and forty thousand horsemen galloped by and I followed them triumphantly.

Skunk appears, tucking in his shirt. As he approaches the car, followed by Clarrie, Bert and Ted laugh in the back seat.

'Whad'di tell ya? He smelt it!' roars Bert. 'Don't get in here. Get in the front. I'm not shiftin' the bottles again.'

Clarrie gets in beside me and Skunk sits on the outside. This is the olden days when the front seat of a cab fitted two people as well as the driver. And a cab was licensed to carry five passengers. Or four passengers and a dozen and a half tallies.

'Whatcha been doin'?' asks Skunk.

'Drinkin' at the Alderley with Ernie.'

'That mongrel,' observes Skunk. 'He's a fuckin' germ! He have that moll with him?'

'What!' exclaims Clarrie, and then for emphasis, 'WHAT!?' He turns to me confidentially. 'He owes four hundred dollars and Ernie's a germ. How do you like that? Four hundred dollars, and he calls him a germ!'

I attempt to repay Clarrie's confidence by trying to understand his meaning, but I can't. With alcohol as their fuel, this group of friends, if you could call them that, continue their impenetrable Sunday night ritual. Insults, laughter, the promise of piss, a journey to someone else's place to drink and argue into the night. Do they have real jobs? Are they going to have to be on deck at seven o'clock tomorrow morning? Will they make it?

Clarrie turns to the new arrival. 'You're a bloody beauty, you are. You owe me four hundred dollars, and you call some cunt a germ!'

'No, don't tell me,' adds Bert, 'don't tell me! Four hundred? It was two hundred last Friday. One born every minute.'

I hear a few chuckles from old Ted in the back, who also passes some inaudible comments before relaxing into a quiet snooze as the conversation subsides for a moment. There's something strange about his being older than the rest. Four men on the loose on a Sunday night, going to visit someone presumably like themselves in a Spring Hill boarding house with eighteen bottles of beer, intent on having a good time. The other three are young enough not to be married or have children or responsibilities, but Ted looks like everybody's father. He has about him the air of a foreman. The very man who will be watching the clock and shaking his head disapprovingly as youngsters like these turn up for work in the morning, hung over and useless. But for now at least, here he is, one of the larrikins. My curiosity's aroused. I want to ask him about his life. He snoozes, mutters something, snoozes again.

Clarrie continues to offer a comment every now and then to me, as an interpreter of their esoteric conversation. There's usually one in every carload of drinking blokes who exhibits a critical awareness. He directs his attention to the driver at certain points, to explain things for him and see how he's getting along. And a driver has to be ready to make use of such an interpreter if things go bad. He will be the one who either pays the fare or collects the money to do so.

As we enter Spring Hill, Brisbane's inner-city residential area, I am reminded of how it's being slowly devoured by the developer's greed. Many fine old houses have disappeared, to make way for impersonal, ugly structures to serve the growth of business. Others have been turned into rabbit warrens to house the large number of people uninterested in the lure of the suburbs. There are still many old double-storey dwellings, wooden or brick or a convenient mixture of both, populated by lonely men, old and shuffling, middle-aged and disillusioned, young and unprosperous. Slavs and Poles. Anglo-Irish. Balkan refugees. Migrants from the old world, still out of place in the new. Men with no families. They work in a variety of jobs, many on night shifts in occupations which carry great responsibility but provide little recompense. They resurface roads on bridges and freeways, sweep floors in hospital wards, clean buses and trains after passengers have deserted them and gone to their warm family homes and roast dinners. These factotums performing essential but unnoticed services bend and crack under the weight we put on their shoulders, and nobody will thank them, least of all the suits at the far end of George Street.

We go down a narrow back street and finally arrive at the rear entrance to Kanga's place, a typical two-storey boarding house with a concreted backyard. Washing lines, propped up by forked sticks, carry the usual flags of convenience – grey-white singlets and work shorts, the odd pair of jeans, an array of blue-collar shirts both short-sleeve and long-sleeve, other simple male attire. No female presence is indicated in this domain. A laundry, half enclosed, half open, surrounds the back steps. There is one modern white washing machine contrasting oddly with the remnants of a bygone era – a green enamel boiler, chipped, stained and useless, the decaying hulk of an old Hoover twin tub, concrete washtubs sitting on a less than horizontal wooden bench with bricks packed under one end where the original support has rotted away.

There are the usual jokes about who pays the fare. Skunk, lured on by the promise of piss, is the first to get out. A few notes are thrust towards me from the back seat. Clarrie collects them and reaches into his pocket for more, and Bert cradles his dozen and a half out of the back seat.

'Here, I'll take the half-dozen,' offers Skunk.

'She'll be right,' counters Bert, in the proprietorial manner of a pilot who intends to see the journey through before his charges safely disperse.

Clarrie, paying the fare, jokes about whether Kanga will be glad to see them. 'Reckon we'll get the turf, driver? Come back in half an hour and we'll be sittin' over there,' he laughs, pointing to a low wall on the opposite side of the laneway. Then he leans over confidentially and begins to say, 'I'll tell you somethin', mate, these cunts…'

But he couldn't finish. The night was split by a painful sound which took an immediate toll on his consciousness – the breaking of bottles. Bert had dropped the entire load of beer on to the concrete, just feet before reaching the back steps. Carrying too many things, he had let the load slip, and then in an effort to save the falling bottles, he'd grabbed for them in such a way that the cartons were flipped over and all eighteen bottles were smacked sideways and upwards, then came crashing down individually on the unforgiving surface of the backyard. Perhaps, I thought, Moses didn't throw down the stone tablets in anger but merely dropped them accidentally as he got out of a cab.

Ted, who had been forgotten, woke with a start in the back seat, looked out, appraised the situation and began to shake his head as he leaned forward to Clarrie and me. 'I have seen the Mortal Sin!' he pronounced. And again, slower, 'I have seen THE Mortal Sin!' In a half swoon, he began to hobble out of the car.

Clarrie began immediately to laugh, in huge bursts. Each burst of laughter fanned the flames of absurdity and his laughter increased. He doubled up. I began to laugh by infection. We were united in our common recognition of the untrustworthiness of the universe. Proof of our rodent nature.

In the courtyard, however, there was no such laughter. All was still, a photographic tableau. Bert stood, incredulous, with the jagged and soggy mess of cardboard and broken glass at his feet, the beer by now finding the lowest point of the yard to trickle towards, returning to the earth from whence it came. Ted plodded around, mumbling incoherently. Skunk simply faded out of sight. Back to Eureka Street, probably, now there was nothing left to drink. A collection of lonely old Slavs and Poles appeared on the lower and upper verandas, eyeing

Bert's tragic figure. They were hushed and curious, deferring to this stranger's grief.

Bert watches the beer flow across the gentle slope of the concrete, under the washtubs, into the drain. He bends down, and places a tentative finger in the rubble, lifts aside the carton, and… Yes! One bottle has been saved! He stands erect, holding the bottle in his hand, tenderly at first, like a flower.

I wait for a whoop of joy.

Suddenly, he hurls the bottle against the wall above the washtubs. It explodes with a thud and a tinkle.

'You fuckin' bastard!' he yells, as the beer runs down the wall and into the tubs. Then he kicks the ruins at his feet.

Clarrie's laughter by now is maniacal. Bert kicks more savagely. Broken glass and flying pieces of soggy cardboard go everywhere.

He keeps kicking, kicking, kicking. 'Bastard!' he yells, 'BASTARD!' and the Slavs and Poles begin to murmur among themselves.

Clarrie, still laughing but trying to hide it from Bert, gets out of the cab and leans against the fence. He laughs, coughs, laughs, then goes into a paroxysm of coughing. He doubles up, falls against the fence, slides down. He sits on the ground with his back against the fence. Bert looks at him. His coughing subsides. Still now, he looks back at Bert.

Bert has nothing substantial left to kick, so he goes over to the back steps of the boarding house and sits down. He puts his elbows on his knees and his head in his hands.

A bloke appears on the upper veranda, wearing thongs, shorts and a singlet, his mouth wide open as he looks down on the scene of carnage and destruction. 'Bert!' he shouts.

This must be Kanga, I suppose, as I quickly execute a three-point turn to make my escape.

Suburban Odyssey

The Treasury Hotel was closing its doors and the patrons were leaving.

I was the first cab on the Treasury rank. In my rear-vision mirror I saw two men come out of the Treasury Hotel and begin to stagger across George Street, carrying a carton of Fourex.

They had that familiar, halting waddle, that deliberate placing of the foot, that careful attempt at containment of undisciplined limbs, which I recognised as the essential behavioural elements of the Australian Drunk. I had been observing drunks since childhood. Out of the pub, on to the footpath, looking around for a cab rank, with that desperate look that says, 'A cab! A cab! My kingdom for a cab!'

There were no other fares evident in the street and the radio was quiet. I was cynical enough to believe that the two drunks would get into my cab, not into the first one they would encounter, at the rear of the rank. I sat, waiting.

An old taxi driver once described to me the awful moment when, stopped in traffic, he looked into his rear-vision mirror and saw a car approaching too fast to stop in time. He knew what would happen and could do nothing but brace himself for the inevitable crash.

So I was helpless for that awful moment. I lost sight of them briefly as they crossed over the street and weaved through the long line of vacant cabs waiting behind me, making me think they might have either disappeared, or become someone else's problem. But suddenly I was startled by urgent knocking on the window behind me.

'Open the boot, mate. Put the carton in.'

It was them all right.

There was plenty of room in the cab for a carton of beer without opening the boot, and I almost said so, but something told me that this perspiring, aggressive drunk had a reason to lock the booze away. Sometimes you just do as you're told.

I got out and opened the boot while he looked on. He carefully placed the carton inside. Twelve large bottles of bitter ale, the best brew in the country. This man's name was Keith, I later discovered. As the evening was to develop, I would get to know him quite well.

His mate, equally pissed but not as aggressive in manner, stood by, even cowered, silently.

'They'll be right in there, Spence,' said Keith, referring to the precious cargo. 'I'll give you half a dozen when we get to your place. Now, let's get goin', driver!'

I was just the tiniest bit afraid of this big loud drunk as I started the engine and turned for instructions to the back seat, where they had both sat, against all bloke-like convention.

Taxi etiquette for blokes. The proper thing for two blokes to do upon getting into a cab is as follows. The one who's going to pay the fare and tell the driver where to go and which way to get there (if he knows), sits in the front seat, beside the driver. The other bloke sits in the middle of the back seat, ignoring the seat belt (which is always deeply embedded in the crease, anyway, along with the five-cent coins and the torn pieces of losing betting tickets). This bloke leans forward a lot of the time to carry on an animated conversation with the other bloke (and the driver, if possible) about football, women, racing or alcohol – obscuring the driver's rear view.

But this unconventional seating arrangement decided upon by my two blokes was merely an indication that I was about to experience a very unconventional journey.

Plan of the voyage…

'Now driver, we're goin' to West End first, to drop me mate off, then I'm goin' on to Salisbury. And I want you to stop off at a florist on the way.' This was Keith speaking, in the voice of authority, even though from the back seat.

'A florist?' I repeated, with surprise. 'Listen, mate, it's after ten o'clock. You won't find a florist open.'

'PLEASE, DRIVER!' he insisted, with raised finger, in a way that would not allow a reply.

Here was an aggressive drunk demanding the impossible after pub-closing time – the stuff that really nasty incidents are made of. Suddenly I felt weak and alone. My mind immediately reviewed tactics.

Surprisingly, I came up with something plausible before too long. 'Okay mate, if we pass a florist that's open, I'll stop.' It's always better to agree in the first instance and hope they'll forget the promise by journey's end.

'Good on yer, mate,' Keith replied, adding gratuitously, 'and if we see any that's closed, we'll blow the bloody horn till they open up again!'

'Well, I don't think they live on the premises, florists, do they?' I felt obliged to say, to test the determination behind his suggestion.

'Some of 'em must. You'd be able to knock 'em up, wouldn't you?' said Keith.

'Well, you can try knocking them up if you like,' I added. 'I'm not leaving the cab unattended.'

'What?'

'Against the rules,' I said, bluffing.

'Well, we'll see…' Keith trailed off.

The journey begins…

Down Melbourne Street, on the short hop to West End, there was a decided lack of open florists. Brisbane has never been the kind of place where people say it with flowers after five p.m. In fact, even after being the centre of the world's attention several times since MacArthur made it his Pacific War headquarters in 1942, the city still goes quiet early in the night. Except for twenty-year-old posers who hang about the trendy nightclubs and can be found seriously inebriated and dangerous, wheeling each other round nearby streets in delinquent supermarket trolleys at three a.m. Young people know how to have fun!

Apart from such self-conscious attempts by the young and reckless to subvert the established order, there is little life to be seen on suburban streets after ten o'clock. Probably because all the life is in cabs, like this one, I remarked sarcastically to myself as the smell of alcohol from the breath of these two brooding beasts in the back seat threatened to knock me unconscious. I rolled down all the windows I could reach without taking my eyes off the road or both hands from the wheel.

By the time we reached the poky West End side street where the back seat bloke was to get out, the concept of florists had been overshadowed by an argument which had developed between these two good buddies about the ownership of the beer in the boot. It was a familiar theme at this time of night, and so I thought it best to simply open the boot and let them sort it out. Five minutes rest, with the meter on detention time. I sat back behind the wheel, cut the engine, and waited to begin the next part of the journey.

However, the muffled sounds of their argument gave no indication of an easy solution. Their discourse grew louder and more distinct.

'Jesus, Keith, I never thought I'd see the day you got dirty over half a dozen bottles.'

'Now, Spence, fair's fair, mate. I paid for the bastards.'

'Bullshit, Keith. I give you the eight dollars when we left the bar.'

'Pig's arse! You gimme four dollars.'

'Eight! Half a dozen are mine!'

'I'll let you have three.'

'Six!'

'Three!'

'I'll fight you for the dozen.'

'You're on!'

I couldn't believe my ears. All I needed was a fight between two passengers in the humid stillness of a summer evening with the journey incomplete and the fare unpaid.

Motivated by the faintest hint of reluctance in their verbal gauntlet-throwing, I decided to act. I took a deep breath and walked round to the back of the car where the men stood, rolling up their sleeves and Jack Dempseying towards each other in the dim glow of the parking lights.

'Now, come on, fellas,' I uttered, with false bravado, 'I'm not having a fight between two passengers while the meter's running. I'm the captain of this ship!'

This was just how bar-room brawls originated: some do-gooder tries to intervene and make peace, but only widens the conflict. I'd seen it in the movies. The adrenalin was racing through my veins. They both stopped and looked at me. I suddenly realised I had left myself open to attack from both of them. As well, the absurdity of what I had just said began to dawn.

After a few tense seconds, they both relented, obviously glad of an official-sounding excuse from a disinterested party to save themselves the bother of a silly duel. Peace with honour.

'All right, Spence. Enough's enough. Here, I'll give you three bottles and we'll hear no more about it,' said Keith, with questionable largesse.

Meanwhile, I took pleasure in my newly discovered diplomatic potential.

Spence, not wishing to risk any further dishonour, quietly agreed and disappeared, although grumbling, with his consolation prize.

Keith meanwhile, glowing from his moral victory, decided it was time to put the carton on the back seat. He sat in the front like a proper bloke should and announced, 'Now, driver, I'm goin' to see a sheila in Salisbury. Got it written down here somewhere…'

He fished in his pockets and handed me a business card with something scribbled in pencil on the back. Merle. Such and such a number, such and such a street, Salisbury. As I handed the card back to him I noticed, printed on the front: New Paradise Health Studio. Massage and sauna, all hours.

'Now, driver, I want to stop and pick up some flowers before we get there.'

He hadn't forgotten. Damn!

'Look, mate, you won't find a florist open this time of night.'

'PLEASE, DRIVER!' The raised finger, again.

I decided to try diplomacy once more. Divide and rule. 'All right, mate. If we see a florist open, I'll stop for sure. You watch that side, I'll watch this side.'

We set off.

Relentless, adrift…

My hastily suggested idea of a dual lookout blunted the edge of his insistence for a mile or two, but he didn't seem likely to forget his request, so I tried hard to come up with a compromise.

'Look, mate, why don't you take her a box of chocolates? We probably won't find a florist open at this hour. Box of chocolates is as good as a bunch of flowers any time.' I tried to make this relatively mundane idea sound as exciting as I could. Sometimes you find yourself telling barefaced lies, unashamed.

'Chocolates?' he queried. Then he subsided for a while, presumably with the image of himself arriving thus laden at her door.

I sensed that the image satisfied him. I had never actually visited a woman with either flowers or chocolates myself, being part of a more cynical and rebellious generation, but I had simply dipped into race memory to drag this idea up. Either that or films I had seen. Keith was a 1950s sort of bloke, anyway, with his sculptured sideburns and his Elvis Presley looks, so the social ecology was all falling into place as this cab load of misfits got propelled into the darkness of the Brisbane night.

As we travelled a stretch of Ipswich Road where there was no danger of finding a florist dead or alive, I observed him for a while, casting intermittent glances sideways as he made himself more and more at home in the front passenger seat.

He was staring straight ahead, expressionless. A sort of ageing bodgie. Or perhaps even older. Had he grooved to Bebop during the late forties and early fifties in the milk bars of urban Australia, I wondered. As with most passengers, I was developing a strange, short-lived intimacy with this Brilliantine-haired relic of the social epoch just before mine. Well, intimacy might be too strong a word. Interest, at least.

Thrown together on life's rough seas…

Front-seat passengers are short-term captives. You watch their faces, you see resemblances to other people you have known, you wonder about their past lives. Occasionally they surprise you completely, contradicting your first impression of them by things they say, attitudes they manifest. They often contribute to your understanding of the great human mysteries, in unexpected ways.

'There's a milk bar just down from Chardon's Corner,' I suggested, musing to myself that it might even have been one of the haunts of his teenage years. The sort of café where he might have fed a jukebox and heard the rhythm and blues that would greatly influence his musical tastes and even his social expectations for the rest of his life. 'They're always open late. They've probably got chocolates,' I added.

Keith grunted affirmatively.

With relief, and a growing sense that this one wasn't going to get the better of me, I pulled up at the milk bar. Yes, I had sold him the idea. He was under control. He went in to examine the confectionery shelf.

It had been a long, hard day, and this was definitely my last fare. I was looking forward to the end of this journey, and sleep.

I half dozed until I heard someone say, 'Where do you want these?'

'What?' I uttered.

'The eggs. Where will I put 'em?'

A shopkeeper in a stained white apron was holding a large open carton of thirty eggs, the sort of thing you see being bulk-delivered to cafes and hamburger joints. 'Bloke said to put 'em in the taxi.'

All suddenly became clear. I'd picked up the human equivalent of a bower bird. 'On the back seat, mate,' I said to the shopkeeper. Beside the beer carton.

This cock was not only gathering a range of gifts to impress his hen when he arrived, but presuming he was going to be invited to stay for breakfast as well. Big breakfast! But I hadn't seen anything yet. Keith came out to the car and showed me two large blocks of chocolate.

'Fruit 'n' Nut and Coconut Rough. Do you reckon these'll do, driver? They haven't got any boxes.'

'Yeah, beaut, mate, I reckon she'll like them,' I said, as convincingly as I could.

He threw the chocolate bars on the back seat between the eggs and the beer.

'You ready to go?' I asked, turning the ignition. I was getting really tired of this fare, and Salisbury was not far off. Soon I would be free to go home.

'Just a minute, mate. Got some fish 'n' chips comin'. I was feelin' a bit hungry. You hungry? I could get him to throw in an extra piece of fish.'

'No… Thanks.' I turned off the ignition and resigned myself to waiting. I was beginning to get the feeling that I would never again be in control of my own life. That I would spend the rest of my days traversing the city at all hours of the day and night and stopping and starting and stopping and waiting, at the whim of people completely unconnected with my real life.

After a further interminable wait, he came back to the car. I no longer anticipated with glee the fat fare at the end of this journey. Distance and waiting time, and their eventual translation into cash, are usually the only elements that can persuade a taxi driver to endure the boredom or the annoyance factors represented by such passengers as the egregious Keith. However, in this case, I just wanted out. But I had no legally defensible grounds to terminate the journey.

Oh, I thought, if only the sleeping citizens in the suburban grid surrounding this late night café, this mere pinpoint on the map of greater Brisbane, were awake, and aware of the courage, the fortitude, the sense of service, the sacrifice, that goes on in the front seats of the thousand or so hacks which ply these unrewarding streets around the clock! How they would respect and revere these selfless servants of the community!

The end in sight...

Keith was positively jolly as he got back into the front passenger seat, rounding off the last bit of repartee with the café owner, who stood, in his greasy white apron, waving him off.

Keith had a large parcel of fish and chips, and a lemon. 'Thank you, driver,' he intoned as he settled back into his front-seat command post.

He had changed. No longer the fighting drunk prepared to draw blood over three bottles of beer, no longer demanding the impossible, but quiet and respectful. Keith was about to meet his Salisbury sheila at long last, and he was mellowing appropriately, before my very eyes. Quite a change from the original intention to arrive romantically, bearing flowers. This tired warrior would be calling on his sweetheart, if indeed she was that, with nine bottles of beer, thirty eggs, two bars of chocolate, a parcel of fish and chips, and a lemon.

'Feelin' a bit peckish, driver,' he said as he unravelled the butcher's paper. 'Got a penknife?'

'No. What do you want a penknife for?'

'Cut the lemon.'

There was no stopping him. He bit the lemon open with his teeth and ravenously attacked the seafood.

'Got a bottle-opener, mate?'

'No.'

'Well, can you just stop over there for a minute?'

He took a bottle from the carton, got out of the car, opened the beer using the two-hand-quick-hit method on a low wooden fence surrounding a park, and got back in.

'Thank you, driver.'

By now I was ready for anything. As we completed the last half-mile of the journey, Keith was contentedly chewing on a prawn cutlet and guzzling a cold ale. I was really looking forward to the end of my shift.

I pulled up outside the designated house in a cul-de-sac in Salisbury. 'There are no lights on,' I observed.

'Geez, this don't look too good,' he said as he went to ring the doorbell. He stood there for something like five minutes, alternately ringing the bell and knocking.

I began to desire sleep with a passion. The ticking of the meter and the promise of eventual payment were losing their relevance to me.

Finally, as lights came on in surrounding houses and inquisitive heads appeared at windows, Keith got the feeling he should stop knocking. There is a certain silent sanctity that settles, along with the dew, on such streets as these after ten at night.

He came back to the car. 'Can't understand it, driver. She said she'd be home. I rung her from the pub.'

'Well, where do you want to go to now?' I asked, no longer able to hide my tiredness, and silently cursing Merle for giving him the bum's rush and spoiling my night.

'There's someone across the street. They might know where she is.'

Keith had spotted a couple in a parked car. He strode over to them, taking them by surprise. Suburban Boy was delivering Suburban Girl home after the pictures and they were sitting in the front seat of his car, talking, or perhaps doing something even more intimate, before she would get out to cross the dewy front lawn of her parental home. I could almost sense Suburban Mum and Dad awake and waiting, with the lights out, for Daughter to return safely.

But Keith rudely interrupted this innocent pre-nuptial scene. Suburban Girl shrieked. Boy grunted with surprise, thinking perhaps it was Her Dad, about to shine an embarrassing torch on aroused passions. Keith had a way of coming up behind people in cars, as I already knew.

I heard the muffled sounds of their conversation. No, they didn't know where the woman from number forty-eight was. They didn't even know her.

But Keith had corollary questions which went on for ever, and I sensed that the young couple were getting more and more nervous under interrogation from a complete stranger with alcohol on his breath and still a touch of aggression – if you didn't know him, like I did. Perhaps Keith was getting envious in the presence of such heterosexual harmony and it made him angry that his suburban girl had apparently given him the flick.

Boy and Girl could take it no longer. I distinctly heard the words 'Bugger off, mate.'

Suburban Mum and Dad could take it no longer, either. I saw the lights come on in their house. The young couple stiffened. What would be next? The sudden appearance of searchlight-equipped helicopters overhead? The abrupt deployment of the tactical response team? Gun barrels poking in at them from every window of their well preserved pale green EH Holden sedan?

Chastened by the Boy's rebuke, Keith walked back across the road, quietly cursing the insolent pup, to report to me. His quest was far from over. 'Shit, mate, beats me. I think I'll try the back door. Just wait a minute, will ya?'

He disappeared down the side of the house. Through the stillness of the night, I could hear his bare knuckles shaking a fly screen door. Then silence.

'Merle! You there, Merle?'

Silence again. The fly screen rattled some more. Lights came on again in the surrounding houses. I checked the meter and tried very hard to convince myself that all this was worth the money.

Keith came back to the cab. 'Well, I'll be buggered. Looks like I've been stood up. Bought the bitch chocolates and everything! Glad we didn't get the flowers now, eh, driver? Least I can eat the chocolates. Would you like some yourself? Will I open the Fruit 'n' Nut?'

'No, thanks. What do you want to do now?' I asked, curtly.

'Just let me think for a minute, driver.'

He sat on the front seat, with the door open and his feet on the kerb. I observed him again. I wouldn't normally spend much time with men like Keith. Our paths would not cross were it not for this occupation I had temporarily chosen. If I had met this same Keith, staggering drunk down a dark street late one night, I would have been frightened. But now, sharing the front seat of a taxi, there was a strange sort of male bond between us. Two blokes, looking for a sheila and sharing confidences in the middle of the night. Well, to put it more accurately, one bloke doing all that and the other bloke observing him, while waiting to be paid so he could go home to bed. I felt no moral obligation to Keith, only a legal one, as described in the precise terms of the Transport Department regulations covering the hire of vehicles within a thirty-kilometre radius of the GPO.

But our being thrown together like this in such a random and in some ways voluntary fashion illuminated awkward truths about the human condition to which both morality and legislation were irrelevant.

The moment of truth…

'I dunno, driver. I'm sick o' this fuckin' life. A man tries to do the right thing, he ends up in the shit.'

'What do you mean?'

'I just can't seem to get on with women. This one…' his hand gestured broadly at the house of the absent (or perhaps merely silent) Merle, but encompassed all women, all houses, all scenes of domestic stability, '…she was a goer. You know…?'

I didn't know, but I nodded.

'She was a goer. She had a bit of life in 'er. She said "Come round and see me at home." She was different to the others.'

'Which others?' I felt obliged to ask.

'The others at the New Paradise.'

'Oh.'

'Don't look so shocked, mate. I'm not ashamed to admit the sort of women I hang around with…'

'I wasn't shocked, I just…'

He sighed and relaxed into the seat. 'Man gets to my age and still alone, he feels like a pork chop in a synagogue. You know what I mean? Lonely. Heartache, stiff-dick fuckin' lonely!' It was a cry from deep down.

I nodded again.

He went on. 'You feel like a turd on the footpath. Everyone walks around you. They avoid you. So when you meet someone like Merle, who shows a bit of interest, you get to thinkin' your life might be worth somethin' after all.' He gazed accusingly at the silent house of Merle the would-be saviour. 'Now this… They just treat you like – dhaaa! I dunno… A man's a fuckin' fool for trustin' 'em.'

Where to start?…

I was chained to this man, now. Bonded. We had lived through the late-night confidences about women which, once uttered, according to the unwritten male lore, call upon each man to energetically support his fellow without question.

But I was kicking against the chains. I wanted to sympathise with this lonely fellow creature, but I couldn't bring myself to say anything as provocative as 'Come on, mate, don't you think you should accept some of the responsibility for your own situation?' But I knew that even if I wanted to, it was neither possible nor worth the effort to change Keith's basic concept of sexual commerce.

The social revolution is much, much harder than the political revolution, I found myself thinking, in contradiction of what I had believed some years before. Then, in the days of protest about what the Americans were doing to Vietnam, many of us thought that changing people's attitudes was the easy task and storming the palace was the one you really needed courage and brilliant organisation for. But now, I reflected, after years of moving implacable and immutable human cargo round the streets of just one small city in the Western world, it seemed tragically clear that putting up the barricades was by far the easier job. Or, as the wise old taxi driver of the rear-end collision described earlier might say, you can't drive up a one-way street the wrong way.

I couldn't think of a thing to say that would console him without actually giving the impression that I concurred with his attitude to women or to life in general. I had talked with other men, my friends, about women, but it was always different to this. We had noted the appearance of Germaine Greer and the others, even if we hadn't read their books. Keith and I belonged to different cultures, different generations. I discovered bebop only through the artificial means of historical research.

We both sat and stared blankly into the night.

After a while he reached for his zip and announced, 'I gotta have a piss.' The time for sensitivity had passed.

I wondered for a few moments about the training which had taught me that logic and reason were the proper basis for action and thought. Sometimes it might be easier and less fraught with angst to just go with the blokes, to agree with everything they say. But I had a memory of being disturbed overhearing a smutty conversation when I was a small boy. It was in the toilet at the Alhambra picture theatre at Stones Corner during interval at the Saturday arvo matinee. Dormant all those years, the memory came flooding back to me with the force of its original impact. I remembered the feeling of extreme danger conjured up in my mind while listening to a fleeting exchange of an anarchic and antisocial nature between two men (they could have just been older boys – one of them could well have been Keith himself) standing on either side of me at the urinal. Their penises protruding, emitting strong jets of urine at the white porcelain in front of them, they vilified several things I had been taught to revere, in a mere two dozen words. I felt embattled, put upon, and even though neither of them would have given my presence a moment's thought, I felt they had the potential to drag me down to a life of unspeakable acts should I acquiesce in their attitude for even a micro-second. This, it seemed to me, was what men did. Crude, hairy, sweaty men. They were forceful,

noisy creatures who talked dirty and pissed with a strong jet that made
a loud noise as it hit the wall of the urinal, creating froth in the trough
below. They were also obliged by the unwritten code to accompany this
physical action with a loud stream of verbal filth on a range of topics.
Nothing was taboo. As a young boy I was terrified, and I knew enough
about logic, reason and gentlemanly behaviour to realise I had strayed
into the path of evildoers.

And so, as Keith announced it was time for a piss, touching off this
cameo memory sequence and signalling that the time for confidence-
sharing had passed, he surprised me by getting up and doing it right
there, beside the cab, on the footpath, outside Merle's house. It also
surprised Suburban Boy and Girl, not to mention her parents and all
the other local residents who by now must have been secretly watching
this circus with interest from behind their respectable curtains.

It was an operation that seemed to go on forever. Apart from the
sound of the piss hitting the grass of the footpath, there was no other
noise in the vicinity, except the ticking of the taxi's meter. Soon, the
volume of production was enough to make the sound of running water
in the gutter quite audible.

Keith looked around and barked at me, 'Hey! Turn the light off,
mate!'

'You left the door open, you idiot…' I almost said aloud.

I was surprised at the anger welling up in me. It could have been the
memory of the Alhambra incident, or the demand Keith was making
on me for a sympathy I was unable or unwilling to provide, but I
checked my anger just in time. I decided not to argue but to simply
lean across and close the passenger door, extinguishing the interior
light. Keith was thereby obscured, but the torrent continued to roar. I
marvelled at the capacity of his bladder.

I also considered driving off and forgetting the fare. But I was in
too deep. So was Keith, in a way. I took great joy in the reflection that
without me he would have been stranded here in a hostile land. He
needed me as much as I needed him.

I saw Suburban Girl chastely kiss Suburban Boyfriend and get briskly out of the car to begin her journey across the parental lawn. Mum and Dad turned the lights out. All was safe.

Keith eventually finished his marathon piss and was standing there, shaking the last drops off, as Boyfriend's car started up, his headlights sweeping round, threatening to illuminate my passenger's dancing organ.

This might have been sweet revenge for Boyfriend, but it could have shocked the neighbours and sent them to their phones to complain of a flasher stalking the streets. Keith zipped up, however, just in the nick of time. The offending part was safely concealed and I fancied I heard the suburban sentinels all around me breathe a collective sigh of relief from behind their venetian blinds.

A new beginning…

Keith came back to the car. 'I decided what I should do. Take me to Mount Gravatt, driver.'

'Mount Gravatt!' I wailed. Was I never going to be released from this nightmare?

'No, I've got a good mate there. He'll put me up for the night.'

If he'd said, 'Back to the city,' I would have been more than pleased. But no, it had to be Mount Gravatt. There's nowhere farther from home than Mount Gravatt at the end of a ten-hour shift. And where would it be when we found his mate wasn't home? Capalaba? Coolangatta? I could see myself driving till dawn.

I broke the land speed record from Salisbury to Mount Gravatt. He directed me to a house in Creek Road.

'There are no lights on,' I informed him, bracing myself for the trip to Coolangatta or some even more inhospitable destination.

'Wait a minute,' said Keith, squinting at the house. 'That's not it. I've forgotten the bloody number, now. You got a torch?'

He got out of the car, with my torch, and went to inspect the diminutive house numbers of one, then a second, and a third house.

He scratched his head. These were originally housing commission dwellings and they were all more or less identical, except for the colour of the paintwork, which in itself was not much of a distinguishing feature at night, under the all-blending glow of fluorescent street lamps, particularly to a tired and emotional drunk.

'They all look the bloody same, driver,' he shouted to me as he walked along the footpath, shining the torch at every house. 'I was only here once, a few years ago.'

Lights were coming on again. In another quiet suburb.

'Keep your voice down, mate,' I felt compelled to say, feeling somewhat responsible for introducing this desperate and lonesome traveller into yet another precinct full of decent, sleeping folk. I drove slowly along the roadway, keeping level with him. I was getting anxious about my torch, knowing the cost of new batteries.

He stumbled and fell on a sunken driveway, losing the torch momentarily. I wondered if I should get out and help him up, but he managed by himself.

Ithaca at last…

Finally, there it was. One of these anonymous, look-alike houses beckoned to him out of dim memory, in the faint glow of the deathly street light.

Keith was overjoyed. 'This is it, driver! I recognise the fence! I remember now. It was on a corner. This corner.'

'There are no lights on,' I found it necessary to say for the third time that evening, and with growing despair.

'No, she'll be right, driver. The car's there. Just hope his old lady doesn't wake up. She's a bloody wowser. She smelt the drink on me last time I was here and almost kicked me out.'

The entrance to the house was in the side street. Keith was making circling and pointing movements with his hand. This meant that I was to do a U-turn and park in the side street, outside his mate's house, for easy unloading of the various goods he had acquired during his travels.

He crossed the road and went in the gate. He mounted the front steps and hesitated before committing his finger to the doorbell. Would only his mate hear it, Keith wondered, and be able to admit him before the wife could stir, and object?

Perhaps his mate would be a better friend to him than I had been. Perhaps his mate would take him in without the condition of an ideological questionnaire.

A light came on, and so I began to think it might be all right to relax. Maybe, just maybe, this was the end. Keith's homecoming. My longed-for release. I calculated how many minutes it would be before I could rest my weary head on my very own pillow in my very own bed.

I heard the murmur of a welcoming voice and stopped the meter.

Keith came back to the car, thanked me profusely, deposited the torch on the front seat, and paid the fare. 'Alf'll put me up for the night, driver. Geez, it's good to have mates... Now, can you just give me a hand to carry this stuff inside?'

That was breaking point.

'Look, mate, I'm a taxi driver, not a delivery boy!'

'Please, driver...' he insisted, with just a hint of the aggression and strength that had intimidated me earlier in the evening when this saga had begun.

But I knew him too well by now. He couldn't scare me any more, or make me feel responsible for his life, or do anything else to render this other than a business relationship. The vague compulsion I had felt at earlier stages of this journey to bond with this fellow male was now understood. We were not mates, not even destined to be mates if by chance shipwrecked together on a desert island. The fare was paid, the contract completed, the bond between us broken. I was free. I was even reckless.

I found myself shouting at him. 'And to tell you the truth, mate, I'm not even a bloody taxi driver! I'm an actor. And a writer. I'm driving this cab and putting up with being abused and underpaid because I can't find the work I really want to do – the work I love!'

Astonishment causes realignments…

This was all too much for Keith. His jaw dropped. He couldn't handle this declaration of passion from someone who was supposed to be merely rendering him a service for the amount shown on the meter.

'Please, driver… Look, it's been a good fare. The least you could do is give me a hand. I have to get all this stuff inside before his old lady wakes up.'

He was appealing to my generosity. I thought he was going to break down and cry. After my outburst, I felt I could relent a little and still retain my dignity. I had taken a principled stand, I had declared my limits, I felt justified.

'Look,' I said, by way of compromise, 'I'll help you get the stuff out of the cab, and I'll leave it at the gate, but I'm not carryin' it inside the house.'

'Okay, mate. Thanks.'

He was truly grateful. I felt like a mongrel.

'Won't be a minute, Alf!' he said in a loud stage whisper to his perplexed friend, who stood motionless in cotton pyjamas on the porch, wondering what could have possibly gone wrong in the world of blokes to have a taxi driver shouting at a bloke just after the bloke had done the decent thing and paid a large fare without complaint.

When the boat comes in…

I took the carton with the remaining bottles of beer from the back seat and placed it on the footpath, near the gate. Keith gathered the fish and chips (half eaten and hastily re-wrapped), the two unopened chocolate bars (he could pretend they were bought specially for Alf's wife), the thirty eggs (she'd love getting them, it would ease his entry into their domestic haven), the lemon (half of it was still useable), and the empty bottle from his front seat banquet. He stood with this armful, the beer at his feet, not quite knowing which to carry in first.

I got back into the taxi and started the engine for the last journey of the night.

His true Penelope…

Suddenly, another light came on in the house, and a woman's stern voice became clear and audible in the still night. 'Alf! Who's that? If it's your drunken mate, Keith, you can tell him to get back in the cab and go somewhere else. I'm not puttin' up with him again!'

With dismay, Keith heard all this. So, probably, did all of Mount Gravatt. It was so loud and so final that I swear even the silent siren Merle heard it back in Salisbury, behind the treacherous rock of her darkened windows.

Keith stood on the footpath, as motionless as his mate on the porch. He looked at me, looked at Alf, and looked back at me. Alf was overcome with indecision. His mouth opened, but no sound came out.

Then she appeared on the porch, beside her husband, addressing Keith directly. 'You're not bringing that beer into this house, Keith! I warned you last time! Alf hasn't touched a drop in five years, and I'm not going to let you put temptation in his way! Go and stay with your harlots, and drink yourself stupid with them!'

Both men went to water. Obviously, this was not a woman with whom they could argue successfully, no matter how tight their male bonding nor how deep their mutual understanding.

'Just a minute, driver,' Keith implored, as a half-dozen of the eggs fell out of their container and smashed on the concrete path in front of the gate, beside the beer carton. 'I might need to go somewhere else…' He stood there, pathetically becoming the turd on the footpath in fulfilment of his own prophecy.

But I had worked long and hard for my freedom. Nothing could stop me now. I put my foot on the accelerator.

Throwing Up in Toowoomba

The first time in his life that Hal was really and truly in love, the whole affair ended tragically.

Angela, the woman who had captured his affections, had seemed to him perfectly suited to spending the rest of her life with him. She gave him joy and expanded his vision of life's pleasures, even helped in the unprecedented enlargement of his mind.

But Angela dumped him unceremoniously one day while the jacarandas were spreading purple carpets on the grass and everything else in Brisbane seemed to be bursting with optimism. It made him realise why people wrote songs about love gone wrong.

Shortly after the dumping, which hurt him to the core, Hal made a trip to Toowoomba to visit her parents.

In the way of young men nursing a broken heart, he threw himself into this patently useless gesture with a desperate sense of self-importance. Why had she dumped him? He had proved himself a worthy companion, a kind and gentle, even romantic lover. Their relationship was smooth and long lasting. Two years of innocent pleasure and discovery, unlocking emotional responses which Hal had never before witnessed in himself or others at such close range. But now this. This ending, this sudden death, this refusal to continue. Something must have entered her mind and poisoned her against him, he imagined.

It was difficult for Hal to understand. This had been the first time he had experienced such deep joy over a sustained period of time. And now it was the first time for such deep pain.

It had always seemed odd that Angela referred to their relationship as an 'affair', a word more often used to describe a covert extramarital pursuit. Hal thought nothing of it at the time. For the bulk of their relationship, there was unqualified mutual acceptance, no hint of jealousy, no consideration of third parties. No one was going to catch anyone in flagrante delicto. In this setting, calling it an affair seemed to increase the danger, the excitement, the unpredictability, as though there was another partner snooping, waiting to detect infidelity. Maybe Angela needed such a dramatic atmosphere to function in the ways that Hal found so compelling. Or was it a sign that she considered herself so attractive that she imagined that by going with Hal, she had countless other potential husbands, lovers and suitors bristling with jealousy and rage?

And so he found himself on the road to Toowoomba, the city of certainties, to be consoled, and fighting back any suggestion that she had not been, at least for the first year and a half, as much in love with him as he had been with her.

Driving up the range alone, Hal sang all the romantic ballads he could remember, out loud, testing the limits of his resistance to the new experience of real sadness. This was the sort of substitute for rational analysis which one could afford to indulge in only if there was no one else present.

His initial reaction to The Dumping had been to spend day after day alone, while his stomach churned and he consumed little other than brandy and bicarb. He visited the old haunts where they had been so happy together. He walked alone along the streets of memory, savouring the sadness.

But it was the realisation that the great world was still turning without his participation which brought him back to noticing what his friends were saying and doing to make him feel better and help heal his broken heart.

Hence, this utterly hopeless gesture of visiting her parents. Fat lot of good it would do him, but somehow the idea had been implanted in his head that other people's views about Angela could help him to bear the loss of her. So he was determined to go through with it.

Hal had visited Toowoomba often with Angela during the life of their affair, when meeting her parents seemed to be an indication of how grown up and ready for responsibility he was. But this was different. This was after the break-up. This was when they must have been saying to each other, 'Why on earth is he coming up here to see us? Why isn't he pursuing her?' Hal often wondered why he wasn't pursuing Angela, too. As did some of his over-confident male friends, such as Shark, the know-all dilettante and part-time taxi driver.

'Get after her, mate. That's what she wants you to do!' he would say after a few drinks. Because he constantly dealt with the public and saw life in the raw, Shark could speak authoritatively on matters of the heart.

But armchair lovers like Shark weren't there to read her face when she broke off the affair. He didn't see the utter finality in her eyes. Hal was often wrong about many aspects of human life, but he could read certainty in a face.

Shark had said to him, 'If you'd driven cabs for five years like I have, you'd be able to tell the difference between bullshit and the truth when you look into someone's eyes.'

Hal was inclined to accept this as the irrefutable wisdom of the streets until one day he was a passenger in Shark's cab. He suddenly realised the worth of Shark's advice. He blurted out, 'But you never look into people's eyes when you're driving. You're watching the bloody road!'

History is history. All one can do is attempt to understand it once it has happened. And when first love goes wrong, as go wrong it must, one is compelled to go to the extremes of human reaction, if for no other reason than just to find out what degree of self-reproach one is capable of.

Toowoomba hadn't changed. The streets were still full of young hoons in cars parading up and down Ruthven Street, trying to impress young women.

Hal pulled up outside Angela's parents' house in the familiar, leafy

Toowoomba street. They were waiting for him. It was Friday night. He'd telephoned last night and they said they'd be pleased to put him up for the weekend. It was like trying to make the past come back, Hal realised, as he grabbed his overnight bag and started walking towards the door. This is useless. Turn around and go home right now, the voices said.

But, ah, no. The grip was too intense. And there was nothing to go home for. At least to be hanging around the place where she and Hal had had so much fun, where the earth had embraced them, was better than facing the loneliness and despair.

Funny what women can do to you, thought Hal. He remembered the same sense of separation and what it had done to him as a much younger person on the platform at South Brisbane Station.

Hal was leaving to begin a completely new life a thousand miles away at the age of eighteen, just out of school. Some distant relation who had a farm in Victoria convinced his parents it would be a good idea if he spent a year close to the soil, rather than in the dangerous world of universities and intellectual freedom. Hal hated the idea of working on a farm, but loved the romantic notion of travel to far away places.

If Angela was now his first true love, then Betty was his first crush. At South Brisbane, Betty was on the other end of the paper streamer which she had thrown and Hal had caught. Hal knew that when he returned she would have moved into different circles and the excitement of their friendship may never be rekindled. She was on the platform. Hal was on the train. There was a big crowd and lots of other streamers. But the one connecting her and him was a special one. It was the thin ribbon of impossible love, a love that could never be. Hal was enjoying its fragility, its romantic charm. It was the symbol of an innocent, adolescent love which gave him the chance to rehearse for his real life which he thought might start a little later on. It was the chance to pose in many guises, to vicariously experience a panorama of emotions. To be Lawrence of Arabia, to be Humphrey Bogart.

The automatic doors of the train closed on the ribbon. The scissors were grinding but not yet severing this token of grand adventure, this symbol of innocent love. Time, place and emotion were frozen. Then the train started to move, the streamer snapped, Hal saw her face flood with tears, and he felt powerful because he could leave a woman behind, crying, at a railway station. Just like in war movies he had seen. He felt elated.

But that was then. He was eighteen and a real arrogant shit. And this was now.

With his newly gained sensitivity, he concluded that he was still a shit, but a little less arrogant and a bit more convinced of the awesome power of human emotions. He knew this affair was over and he knew why, more or less, but he couldn't come to terms with the fact. On the train all those years ago, he enjoyed feeling the sadness of departure and how it elevated his heroic notion of himself, but now this separation was serious and he desperately craved a resolution.

Angela's younger siblings were there. Her mother, Colleen, was cooking real country food. Her father, Fred, whimsical and inquisitive, was making jokes and drinking beer in the kitchen. It was just like before, only she wasn't there.

Colleen took time off from her meal preparation to show him the spare bedroom where he was to sleep that night. Hal thanked her profusely and put his overnight bag on the bed.

'I won't say I didn't expect it,' offered Colleen.

Hal wasn't prepared to discuss the affair so suddenly. He took a deep breath. 'I suppose I should have seen it coming, but I didn't want to,' he confessed, surprising himself with his own honesty.

'Angela was very happy for the first little while. She used to tell me what a wonderful, interesting man you were…all twenty-five years of you.'

'You used to talk about me?' asked Hal, affecting naivety in the hope it would bring on sympathy and confidence.

'Daughters always talk to their mothers about their boyfriends,' replied Colleen. 'Don't you ever talk to your dad?'

'Wouldn't know where to begin,' admitted Hal.

'You two could never have lasted. It was first love for both of you.'

Hal, still remembering the sweetness of it, protested. 'Why can't first love be last love?'

'That's the rules. I don't know why.'

Colleen was infinitely wise and yet compassionate. Hal had always felt more comfortable with her than with her daughter, even though he would never admit this to anyone.

'Colleen! What's this boiling over, here?' shouted Fred.

It terminated the conversation in the spare bedroom as Colleen rushed back to being a housewife in a country kitchen. Hal followed her back, hoping to continue their talk, but it felt awkward talking about his great love in the presence of Fred, the man, the father. As he looked at Fred, slumped over the racing form on the corner of the kitchen table, he knew how far away and how long ago was the sheer delight of the first time he kissed that man's daughter and looked into her eyes.

'Come down the pub and have a drink,' said Fred. 'Tea'll be a little while yet.'

'Fine,' said Hal. He had never been drinking with her father before. This was real man's stuff, and maybe a way to traverse that long distance.

Colleen winced, but the habits of thirty years' submission to a truck-drivin', hard-drinkin' Irish Catholic Australian husband are hard to break. They left for the pub, in his prime mover.

Hal never realised Toowoomba was such a vast city. They went through a maze of backstreets and arrived at a pub which he had never seen before. A quaint, old, wooden Queensland hotel, with upstairs verandas where men in blue singlets were hanging out their washing and exchanging Zane Greys. He knew something of the Zane Grey world and the quiet pleasures of reading these tales of the American west. His own father had read them constantly. Hal once thought he might try to write a western. They looked easy, and could be a way to make a few bucks. But after typing five pages he was monumentally bored. It had nothing to do with his life.

When they were inside the public bar, Fred introduced Hal to his drinking mates. Tom. Snowy. Bill. This is really the country, thought Hal, a world of solitary men who work hard and drink hard. These boys with boozy faces had been drinking since four o'clock and were pretty committed to the piss by now. Hal had the usual embarrassment of not knowing the drinking lore, and he fumbled in his pocket, wondering whether to buy a round for everybody, or just for Fred. Fred became immediately involved in about five conversations, with his mates, with two men at the other end of the bar, with the barmaid, Connie, and the publican, Ralph. Ralph was a large bald man who sat behind the bar, steadily consuming neat glasses of rum and doing no work. Connie was run off her feet.

'Shall I…?' began Hal, and was immediately embarrassed by the choice of shall instead of will. Even will is a bit pooncey, he thought.

He began again. 'Can I get you a beer?' he said to Fred.

But Fred had already used sign language to order a round for Snowy and the others, as well as himself and Hal. Connie magically appeared with a tray full of pots, not a drop spilt and the right amount of foam on each one.

'Thanks, Con,' said Fred, with a confidentiality and a sincerity which made Hal feel that his own impoverished life lacked the ability to relate to ordinary people.

Connie responded with something Hal couldn't quite hear, but the tone of it placed it firmly within the fabric of a community of human beings all striving in unaffected ways to achieve simple but honest goals.

The noise in the bar prevented audible conversation as Hal had previously known it, but there was something exciting about it. This was how the real world of hard-drinkin', truck-drivin' men communicated on a Friday night.

'Good health,' said Fred as he raised his glass.

Hal took up his beer, acknowledged the toast and drank. He imagined how the first mouthful of beer on a Friday night must taste to a hard-working truck driver, and convinced himself that he was experiencing that very taste. This was the first beer Hal had drunk since The Dumping. It tasted marvellous, he realised.

For a moment, Hal thought of himself as a truck driver living with Angela and the kids just a few blocks away from Fred and Colleen, and coming here to this pub every Friday night with Fred and his mates to humbly learn how to be a bloke.

Snowy cracked a joke, and the whole company laughed. Hal had no idea what the joke was about, but it involved Ralph and Connie, who also were laughing loudly. Hal laughed too, not at the joke, which he didn't understand, but because he was suddenly engulfed in a sea of mirth. The tilting, swaying, foam-capped waves of laughter were all around him, buoying up his little solitary craft and reducing his loneliness in a very short time.

After a while, he felt bold enough to offer to buy a round. He found that by nodding at Connie she understood perfectly what he wanted. For a moment he felt that slightly guilty but comfortable power men often have over women in subordinate positions.

They drank some more, and Hal was really enjoying himself. He thought about Colleen, back in the kitchen preparing a meal for them, and was about to remind Fred, but thought, ah no, Fred will have taken care of that. Any man who can excel in non-verbal communication with barmaids and handle social interaction with these jolly men so deftly will surely know when to leave so as to arrive home in time for tea. I'll leave that to him. I'm in the land of blokes and Fred is the king of the blokes.

But Fred had forgotten about the evening meal in the country kitchen. He was indeed with the blokes. His mates. And Hal was being invited to be one of his mates. Hal had another beer. And another. Soon, he lost count of how many beers he had had, and also of whose round it was. The waves of jollity were crashing all round his little boat. He was awash with foam, with laughter and uncaring.

Conventional time was suspended. Everything was a bit of a

blur. Hal found himself standing at the urinal with Snowy beside him, telling yet another incomprehensible joke. Hal didn't know at which point the punchline had occurred, but when he heard Snowy break into raucous laughter, he did likewise. Suddenly the world was spinning, and Snowy had gone back to the bar. Hal was still standing at the urinal. It occurred to him that he didn't know where he was. A moment ago amid a noisy collection of drinking, bonding males. Now alone.

The cool stainless steel surrounds of the urinal seemed to suggest permanence and redemption as the clean water flushed away the piss. He looked down and saw a rabid collection of soggy cigarette butts fighting to enter the little crevices in the drain cap as the water and urine bubbled and gurgled and made the throttling sounds of escape. Which one of these little sperm will be first to get in and fertilise the egg, he thought. He knew he was pissed.

Hal finished urinating and was zipping up his fly as a faint glimmer of recognition returned. He said to himself, 'I'm in a pub in Toowoomba. I'm drinking with Angela's father. It's Friday night.' At least the booze had taken his mind off his sadness.

Back at the bar, Fred said to him, 'You know where you went wrong?'

'Where?' asked Hal, now ready for anything.

'Where you went wrong, the point where it all went bad, was when you let her get away with not goin' to Mass. That's when the rot set in. You should've said somethin' to her.'

Hal was too pissed by this stage to disagree, or even to point out to Fred how fucking stupid this opinion was, in his view. Here he was on a Friday night in a pub in Toowoomba, listening to a drunk tell him how he mismanaged his relationship to his daughter! Come on, Fred, give us a break, thought Hal. He was not so pissed that he couldn't see that Fred was totally out of touch with his own daughter, not to mention the times.

He was about to launch into a realistic description of Angela's state of mind, her attitude to the Church, her well developed critique of religious superstition, her agnostic cynicism, her broad humanist compassion, her belief in the essential goodness of humanity and the redemptive nature of social action, when he thought better of it, on two counts. The first was that he was too inebriated to do justice to the subject, and the second and decisive count was that it no longer mattered. The affair was over. Telling her father what a wonderful, enlightened, liberating mind she had would only make Hal feel miserable and want her all over again. Fred could die in ignorance. She was gone and Hal would never get her back.

The time went by very quickly, and these two unlikely mates talked of many other topics. Talked, that is, under the conditions of noise level and inebriation described above. Snowy and Bill had gone home, and Tom had found new friends across the room. Hal saw two or three pies placed in front of him over a period of an hour or so, and someone squirting tomato sauce on them. Was it Connie? And he had a vague feeling of guilt that that woman was back in that kitchen preparing a meal for him.

Without remembering the actual words used, Hal was conscious that a collective decision was taken to return home. Fred was at the wheel of the prime mover and Hal could see the back streets of Toowoomba moving past outside the window. At a later time in his life Hal would abhor the elements of this situation, but for now it hardly seemed important that a very inebriated man was driving a heavy vehicle through urban streets, endangering lives. Perhaps road safety was something you could leave off worrying about until you got your human relationships sorted out.

Miraculously, no accident occurred. Fred parked the vehicle safely outside the house. The two males entered the house through the back door. The kitchen was empty, the stove turned off. Colleen was sitting in the lounge, reading.

Fred went in to make his peace with her. Hal heard them shouting at each other as he prepared for bed. He couldn't face Colleen in this condition, and even though he felt guilty about not confessing to his part in the lack of consideration for her domestic labours, he ripped off his clothes and flopped on the bed. Within two minutes he was fast asleep.

He woke suddenly in the middle of the night and wondered, again, where he was. Then, when the unfamiliar landscape of the room gradually told him the answer, he realised he was about to become violently ill. He quickly gathered his trousers and pulled them on so he could make his way to the outside toilet with dignity. A few steps outside the door and he knew he had put his trousers on back to front. But that didn't matter. Shit, he thought, I should have a torch, there's no light in the dunny. But he wouldn't have needed it anyway. Halfway across the well-kept lawn, he threw up, under the Hills hoist.

On his hands and knees, his trousers round the wrong way, and no shirt on in the cool Toowoomba night, he was throwing up by the bucket load. It was a good thing no one was observing this undignified exhibition, he thought.

After he finished vomiting, he sat back on the dewy grass and felt relieved. Clean, almost. The cool air was refreshing him and he felt very sober. But tired. Too tired to clean up the mess. I'll do it in the morning, he thought. He stood up, lowered his back-to-front trousers and had a piss on the lawn. Urine is good for lawns, he reminded himself. Nitrogenous waste. Fertiliser.

In the morning, Hal felt generally better and lay awake for a while, looking at the ceiling. Gradually, realisations began to dawn. The need to make apologies to Colleen for missing tea and for getting drunk with her husband while a guest in her house. He reflected on this and tried to create a form of words which would help him through this difficult task. But the thing that got him out of bed was the need to clean up the vomit under the Hills hoist before the other family members got to see it and be disgusted. Hal dressed quickly and went out to the backyard looking for a shovel and a garden bed that could do with some immature compost.

The lawn, however, was totally clean. There wasn't a trace of evidence. His misdemeanour had already been forgiven, wiped out, erased. The rank smell of vomit had been replaced by the sweet scent of eucalyptus deodorant spray.

Who did it? Someone must have been up very early, he thought. Or had they seen the actual vomiting episode itself in the middle of the night? He really wanted the answers to these questions, but it wasn't the sort of thing he could ask at the breakfast table, 'Hey! Good morning funsters! It's me, the failed suitor for your daughter's hand in marriage. Who cleaned up my vomit under the clothesline? Which one of you silently watched me throwing my guts up last night?'

The aroma of bacon and eggs wafted past his nose. The smell of certainty on Saturday morning in the city of certainties. It superimposed itself on the eucalyptus, even obliterated the memory of the smell of midnight spew.

Colleen was calling out to him, as pleasant as ever. 'Hal! Ready for breakfast?'

'Yes, Colleen. Just coming.'

Breakfast was reassuring, as country breakfasts always are. The conversation ranged widely. Trucking was discussed in detail, as was tennis and rugby league. There was general agreement about the superiority of country eggs over city eggs. The bacon was better, too. City bacon came from the country, it was agreed, but the travelling didn't do it much good. Wine's another thing that doesn't travel well, thought Hal, remembering countless bits of information siphoned from Shark's lounge room lectures on the grape. But before Hal could add this drop of wisdom to the conversation he decided it was better to avoid all mention of alcohol. The tea tasted good, the toast and marmalade was wondrous.

Spirits were high around the table. Hal felt very welcome in this household. Which made him sad, because he had never felt this welcome when he visited here with Angela. And now it meant nothing because he knew it was probably the last time he would visit here. Come to think of it, they must know that too, thought Hal. That's why everyone is being so nice to me. They know they won't have to put up with me ever again, won't have to get up early in the morning and clean up the puke under the hoist. Their daughter won't be married to me, there'll be no connection between me and this family.

As these thoughts caused the tears to well up inside him, Hal fought them back. He kept forcing himself to talk only about happy things, light things. He remembered movies he had seen where the hero was the one everybody else was relying on. He imagined he had to keep everyone else's spirits up.

Pretty soon he found himself laughing and joking, and being able to talk with credibility to Angela's younger brothers and sisters, something he had never been able to do before. The acceptance increased as the realisation became more acute that the relationship with Angela was over. He saw the lonely road back to Brisbane stretch out before him. He had come here looking for consolation and must leave with something less. What was the use of coming, he asked himself again.

Throughout breakfast there was no mention made by anyone of the previous evening. No reference to the boys staying at the pub, to the dried out meals left in the oven, and certainly no mention of the vomit on the lawn. Fred announced that he had to go and look at some equipment for his truck.

'I have some shopping to do,' said Colleen.

'Well, you should've said so,' replied Fred. 'It's too late now. I have to be there in ten minutes, otherwise I'll miss out on the chance of a lifetime.'

Colleen could see there was no way Fred could take her shopping.

Hal jumped in. 'I've got nothing to do. I could take you.'

'Are you sure?'

'Sure,' said Hal. 'I'd love to.'

'Good,' said Fred, as he stood up and extended his hand for Hal to shake. 'Been nice seein' you again, Hal.'

Hal shook the hand of the man who would never be his father in law.

As their eyes met, unspoken messages crossed between them, inarticulate, confused. Both men realised they were dealing with something beyond their power to understand, much less to put into words.

'Thanks, Fred,' Hal finally managed to get out.

'What for?' replied Fred in a way that prevented an answer. Then, because he had no other words, he offered, 'Good luck, mate.'

And he was gone. In his prime mover.

Hal was sick of this. Sick of going through life not being able to talk about what was happening to him. Sick of not being able to talk to people honestly and openly about the unmentionable, the unpleasant, the difficult. There has to be a better time ahead, he thought to himself, when you can be totally straight with people, no matter how ugly the truth between you.

Colleen started getting ready to go shopping. Hal was resigned. He planned how it would be. He would drop her off at the supermarket, arrange to call back for her at a nominated time, drop her home with the shopping, and then go straight back to Brisbane to begin a new and more honest life where he would never more be the slave of questionable social conventions, like last night at the pub.

Angela's brothers and sisters all disappeared to take part in Saturday morning activities. Dancing class, football, model plane building. Hal wished he could have gone with them and participated in these further certainties. But the certainty of shopping is probably just as good, he reasoned, just as reassuring. By the time he had delivered Colleen to the shopping centre, he had decided he might as well come into the shops with her. There was something about pushing a trolley up and down the aisles that promised to make him feel safe and comfortable, in touch with the real world.

The trolley was half full in no time. It always amazed Hal to watch real housewives shopping. They never just got one packet of anything, as do single men living in untidy flats and houses. Housewives grabbed two or three, or the jumbo size. They had a sense of planning, they dealt with economies of scale. They bought ingredients for meals that would occur in several days' time. They bought solid vegetables – pumpkin, potatoes, carrots, celery, onions. They didn't waste time on snow peas and button squash.

In a crowded aisle where Colleen spent some time deciding which bulk detergent to buy, Hal was sent off to get four litres of milk. When he returned, he found Colleen not much farther advanced. She was working off a list. He could sense they were nearly finished shopping as he asked what else he could get for her. He liked the thrill of boundary riding, and coming back to the main party with one or two little items, adding to the weight of the trolley.

'Need any of this?' he asked, not looking, but waving a hand around at their immediate environment.

'Oh, yes, get me one of those,' said Colleen, pointing at a particular shelf. It was not on her list.

Hal looked at what she had just indicated and found to his horror that he was standing in front of the deodorisers and disinfectants. The entire supermarket seemed to come to a standstill. Eucalyptus deodorant air freshener.

He placed it in the trolley. 'Look, Colleen, I'm sorry about…'

'Hush. It's in the past.'

He smiled at her. He fancied he was smiling at Angela. He was about to say, 'It won't happen again,' and then he realised the circumstances would never occur again.

They passed through the checkout and loaded the goods into the car. On the homeward journey Hal began to compose a farewell speech. But when he arrived back at Colleen's house, it all seemed too sentimental, so he said nothing. He helped her take the shopping inside, she thanked him, he grabbed his overnight bag and stood in the doorway.

'Get on with your life, Hal,' urged Colleen. 'You'll meet someone else. In five years' time you'll have forgotten all of this. You'll meet someone and she'll be right for you. You'll forget Angela. You probably won't even remember Fred and me.'

'Thanks, Colleen,' was the only bit of Hal's speech that survived.

'Safe trip,' she said. She kissed him on the cheek.

That was it. That was the end. He now had nothing to do with Angela or her family. Or even with Toowoomba. He had to go on living without them. He felt a sort of relief, tinged with regret. He had to find new friends, busy himself with activity. He braced himself for the expected interrogation by his flatmate Shark: 'Well, do they reckon there's any chance? Do they reckon they can change her mind?'

He would have to tell Shark that there was no chance, that he didn't even try to enlist their help in such a hopeless crusade. He thought once again (was it to convince himself?) of the finality in Angela's eyes when she told him it was over.

The long road down the range and into the Lockyer Valley was even more lonely than it was going up the day before. Hal didn't even bother to sing his favourite songs of loss and thwarted love. He drove silently, staring straight ahead. His gaze was fixed on the unknown future.

He could sense there was value in the wisdom of Colleen's parting words, but he couldn't see it just yet.

He pulled into the parking area of a fruit barn near Marburg, and cried. He sat there for an hour, and cried and cried and cried.

Since the early 1970s Errol O'Neill has worked as an actor, writer, director, dramaturg and producer, specialising in the creation of new work for the Australian theatre. He has published many short stories, written chapters and articles for books and journals on aspects of theatre and society, and guest-lectured in tertiary drama courses. He wrote half a dozen political satires for the Popular Theatre Troupe and has written many plays on aspects of Queensland and Australian history, which have been produced by La Boite, Queensland Theatre Company and other theatres in Brisbane and interstate.